Chelsea Martin Turns Green

Chelsea Martin Turns Green

BECKY THOMAN LINDBERG

Illustrations by NANCY POYDAR

ALBERT WHITMAN & COMPANY
Morton Grove, Illinois

AUG 09 1994

Library of Congress Cataloging-in-Publication Data

Lindberg, Becky Thoman.
Chelsea Martin turns green / Becky Thoman Lindberg;
illustrated by Nancy Poydar.
p. cm.
Summary: Chelsea fears that she is losing her best
friend Mary Lynne to Abigail, the new girl in their
third grade class.
ISBN 0-8075-1134-X
[1. Friendship—Fiction. 2. Schools—Fiction.]
I. Poydar, Nancy, ill. II. Title.
PZ7.L65716Ch 1993   92-31613
[Fic]—dc20   CIP
                                                 AC

Text copyright © 1993 by Becky Thoman Lindberg.
Illustrations copyright © 1993 by Nancy Poydar.
Designed by Susan B. Cohn.
Published in 1993 by Albert Whitman & Company,
6340 Oakton Street, Morton Grove, Illinois 60053.
Published simultaneously in Canada
by General Publishing, Limited, Toronto.
10 9 8 7 6 5 4 3 2 1

To Frank.

Contents

A Job for Chelsea

"**G**reen cupcakes?" said a voice. "That's sick!"

Chelsea Martin had just set a tray of cupcakes on her desk. She whirled around. Arthur Wilmot, the tallest boy in third grade, was standing behind her.

"They're *supposed* to be green," she said stiffly.

Chelsea had hardly spoken to Arthur since the last class party. She had made him a beautiful valentine and signed it "From Your Secret Admirer." But he had crumpled the big red heart and thrown it on the floor.

Now Arthur made a face. "You won't catch *me* eating anything green!"

Humph! Chelsea remembered Arthur stuffing cookies into his mouth at the Valentine's Day party. I bet he'll change his mind, she thought.

She waited for him to move on down the aisle. Instead, he took a creased sheet of pink construction paper out of his pocket. "I want to hire you," he said. "You and Mary Lynne."

Oh! thought Chelsea as she stared at the pink paper. That's one of our advertisements!

One boring Saturday afternoon, Chelsea and her best friend, Mary Lynne Woodlie, had decided to start a business. They'd written out ads and then passed them around at school the following week.

If you need help,
just ask us —
Mary Lynne and Chelsea
We do things you don't
want to do.
And we work cheap!

That had been days ago—weeks even!—and not one job had turned up. Chelsea had almost forgotten about the business.

Now she said, "Well, okay. What do you want us to do?"

"There's. . .there's a girl I like." Arthur's face turned red. "I want you to ask her if she'll be my girlfriend."

Chelsea was amazed; she thought that Arthur hated girls! She was also terribly curious. "*Who* do you like?"

Arthur looked dreamy. It was as if a six-foot-tall Milky Way bar had suddenly appeared in front of him.

"Abigail," Arthur said softly. "Abigail Mac-Cready."

What? Chelsea thought. The new girl? I should have known!

Abigail MacCready had long, skinny legs, red hair, and green eyes. She'd been in Mrs. Findlay's class exactly one week. And already, thought Chelsea, she's taking over the whole third grade!

"Why do you like *her*?" said Chelsea.

Arthur raised his eyebrows. "Haven't you seen her playing soccer? Or doing those jump-rope tricks at recess?"

"Ye-es," Chelsea said glumly, "I've seen her."

Although Chelsea did an excellent job of turning cartwheels and standing on her head, she had never been very good at soccer. And when it came to jumping rope, she was only average.

"Well," said Arthur, "then you can see why I like her. She's terrific at sports!"

"But," Chelsea said, "you can't have a girlfriend—you're too young."

"I am not!"

Chelsea crossed her arms. "Are too! Anyway, getting someone a girlfriend is not the kind of job Mary Lynne and I do."

Arthur raised his eyebrows. "Oh, yeah? Look here." With one finger, he tapped the pink construction paper. "Your ad says, 'We do things you don't want to do,' and that means anything!"

Chelsea frowned. "No, it doesn't mean—"

"Besides," Arthur interrupted. "I'm willing to pay you fifty cents." He reached into his pocket and pulled out two shiny quarters.

I don't care if he offers me fifty dollars! thought Chelsea. I'm not going to get him a girlfriend! But just as she opened her mouth to refuse the money, Mrs. Findlay called the class to order.

"All right!" the teacher said. "The people who brought party food can set it on this table. The rest of you take your seats, please!"

"Here," whispered Arthur as he grabbed Chelsea's hand. He shoved the quarters into it and closed her fingers over them. Then he scurried to his desk in the next aisle.

Chelsea stared at the shiny coins, then dropped them into her pocket. After taking her cupcakes to the front of the room, she sank into her chair. Maybe I *should* talk to Abigail, she thought. Maybe Abigail would *like* to be Arthur's girlfriend.

Chelsea pictured Arthur and Abigail sitting side by side on the playground bench. Maybe Arthur would put his arm around Abigail. Maybe he'd even. . .even try to kiss her!

Ugh! Chelsea shuddered at the thought of Arthur's blubbery lips. Well, she decided finally, she'd have to talk it over with Mary Lynne.

When it was time for recess, Chelsea looked around the playground for someone with black hair and coffee-colored skin. Where *was* Mary Lynne? Oh! She was over there, by the tire swing.

"Mary Lynne!" Chelsea called as she hurried toward her. "I've got to talk to you. Wait till you hear—"

Just then, someone else shouted from across the playground. "Mary Lynne! I'm over here!"

It was Abigail. She stood next to the jungle gym with her neon-green jump rope dangling from one hand. She signaled to Mary Lynne. "Come on!"

Mary Lynne began to run. "I've got to go!" she called over her shoulder. "Abbie promised to teach me how to do Double-Dutch."

"Wait!" Chelsea began. "I didn't get a chance to tell you. . . ." But it was too late. Mary Lynne was halfway across the playground.

Why does Abigail have to butt in every time I'm talking to Mary Lynne? thought Chelsea. Mary Lynne and I have been best friends for years, after all. And Abigail has only known her for one week!

Chelsea stood and watched as the two girls started to jump together. She felt awfully left out.

Sighing, she began to walk toward the line of girls and boys waiting for the tire swing. Then—ooomph!—she felt a thump between her shoulder blades. She staggered forward a few steps, then turned to see who had bumped her.

It was Arthur. He stood there with a big grin on his face. "Did you ask Abigail yet?" he said. "Did you ask her if she'd be my girlfriend?"

Chelsea glared at him. He was so irritating! What right did he have to shove her like that?

She remembered the beautiful red heart she'd made him for Valentine's Day. And she remembered the way he had tossed it on the floor. She'd fix him!

"Yes!" she snapped. "I asked her."

"Yeah? What did she say?"

"She said no!"

Arthur's shoulders slumped. His mouth curved down at the corners. "She did? She said no?"

For a moment, Chelsea felt sorry for him.

"You must not have asked her right!" Arthur declared.

Humph! thought Chelsea. Is that so?

"Yes, I did!" she said. "Abigail just doesn't want to be your girlfriend, that's all."

"Oh," said Arthur.

Chelsea watched him slowly walk away. She felt just a little uneasy. Maybe she shouldn't have said that.

She glanced across the playground. Abigail was still jumping rope with Mary Lynne. What would Abbie say if she knew about the lie Chelsea had just told?

Oh, well, Chelsea thought, I'm not going to worry—she'll never find out!

··2··

The Food Fight

At two o'clock, Mrs. Findlay pushed back her chair, stood, and smoothed the skirt of her green dress. "All right, class, let's get ready for our St. Patrick's Day party."

She asked Mary Lynne to set out paper cups on the table at the front of the room. And it was Chelsea's job to pass out the green paper napkins. Up and down the aisles Chelsea went, and then she reached Arthur's desk.

"Give me back that fifty cents!" whispered Arthur.

Chelsea hesitated. She reached into her pocket to finger the coins Arthur had shoved into her hand that morning.

Why did he want his money back? Had he figured out what really happened—that she had never actually talked to Abigail? Maybe I should give it to him, Chelsea thought.

"Come on!" said Arthur in a low voice. He leaned closer so Mrs. Findlay wouldn't hear. "You did a lousy job, so hand over my fifty cents!"

Chelsea stared at him. A lousy job? She hadn't even wanted the job! He was the one who had made her take that money. And now that he was acting so mean, she wasn't going to give it back!

"Hah!" she said, slapping a napkin down on his desk. "I did not!" She stomped off.

When Chelsea returned to her seat, Mrs. Findlay was assigning people to pass out the party food. There was lots of it, and almost everything was colored green.

Arthur will have to eat green food, Chelsea told herself, or he won't eat anything!

Katie Klein raised her hand. "Where's the lime sherbet I brought in, Mrs. Findlay?"

"Oh! It's still in the freezer." In a firm voice, the teacher added, "Now, I'm going to the kitchen to get the sherbet. I want you all to behave while I'm gone."

The door closed behind Mrs. Findlay. Immediately, Arthur Wilmot popped out of his seat. "Hey, everybody!" He held up one of Chelsea's cupcakes. "Don't eat these—she spit in the icing!"

What! Chelsea rose halfway up from her chair. "I did not!" she exclaimed. She stuck out her tongue at Arthur.

"Did too!" Arthur set his cupcake in the middle of his desk top. He spread his napkin over it. "Watch this!"

An excited murmur rose over the room as everyone turned to look at Arthur. Oh, no! thought Chelsea. I hope he's not going to . . .

Arthur made a tight ball of his right hand. Then—wham!—he brought down his fist.

Smashed bits of cake squirted across Arthur's desk. The cupcake wasn't a cupcake anymore. It was a pancake!

Grinning, Arthur glanced over his shoulder at Chelsea.

Chelsea could not believe what Arthur had just

done. Her own busy mother had taken the time to bake those cupcakes. And Chelsea had iced all of them herself.

She wasn't going to let him get away with it. She looked around for weapons. Ah...here was a plastic spoon and a cube of jiggly lime jello.

Chelsea set the jello on the spoon. Then she held the spoon like a catapult, with the handle down, and carefully pointed it in Arthur's direction.

"Hey!" he said, watching her with big eyes.

Chelsea pulled back on the spoon. Ready... aim...*fire!* She let go, and the cube of jello was hurled into the air—straight toward Arthur!

But at the last minute, Arthur ducked.

Ka-splat! The jello went right into the middle of Thomas's forehead. It stuck there for a second, then slid slowly down to his nose.

"Mmmpf!" exclaimed Thomas. He wiped off his face with a napkin.

Glaring at Chelsea, he scooped up some candy from his desk. "Take that!" he yelled, firing gumdrops at her.

Before Chelsea could do anything, there were

one, two, three bits of candy falling ping! ping! ping! on her arms and chest. "That's not fair!" she said, "I didn't mean to hit *you*, Thomas!"

She tossed one of the gumdrops back at him. "Ow!" Thomas yelped.

Chelsea grinned. She had scored a direct hit!

"You can't do that to my buddy!" yelled Arthur. "Hey, everybody—food fight!" He whirled around and flung a shamrock cookie at Mary Lynne.

For a moment, Mary Lynne just sat there with her mouth open. Then she shook the crumbs out of her hair and armed herself with Cheese Doodles. "Take that!" she said. "Pow! Pow! Pow!"

Thomas dropped a green Gummy Worm down Katie Klein's back. "Eeek!" she yelled. She dug out the worm and pitched it back.

Food was flying everywhere! There was yelling and screaming, and then—suddenly—Mrs. Findlay yanked open the door. A hush fell over the room.

"Tsk, tsk, this is disgraceful!" The teacher looked sternly around at her students.

Uh-oh, thought Chelsea. It wasn't my fault... not exactly. But maybe I shouldn't have gotten so angry when Arthur smashed the cupcake.

Oh, no—now Thomas was pointing right at her. "She started it!" he said.

"Yeah," said Arthur. "It was Chelsea!"

"No," said Mary Lynne. "It was *you*!"

"It was Arthur," agreed Katie Klein.

"All right." Mrs. Findlay took her place at the front of the room. "It doesn't matter who started it. There'll be no recess on Monday because you *all* misbehaved."

"Awww," murmured Arthur.

Chelsea felt her cheeks get hot.

"Now," said Mrs. Findlay, "clean up this food. I've never seen such a mess!"

After school, walking home with Mary Lynne, Chelsea still felt embarrassed. "Everyone hates me," she said, "for spoiling the party."

Mary Lynne shrugged. "Not really. That food fight was a lot of fun."

"Oh." Chelsea felt a little better. Today was Friday, after all. And there was the parade on Sunday to look forward to.

"This year, there's going to be a leprechaun

contest before the St. Patrick's Day parade,"
Chelsea reminded Mary Lynne.

"I know."

"I'm going to enter. Are you?"

Mary Lynne shook her head. "No, my mom said
we don't have time to get a costume together.
But I think Abigail is going to enter."

"Oh," said Chelsea. "You mean she's going to
the parade?"

"Yes, and Chelsea..." Mary Lynne hesitated.
"There's something I have to explain."

Chelsea stared at Mary Lynne. Mary Lynne
wasn't smiling. She looked serious, and she sounded
serious, too.

"Yesterday Abigail asked me to go with her to
the parade," said Mary Lynne, "and my mom
thought it would be nice because Abbie's new in
town. So, anyway, this year I'm going with her."

At first, Chelsea didn't say anything. She was
stunned. She and Mary Lynne always went to
the parade together.

"She doesn't like me," she finally muttered.

"Who?"

"Abigail." Chelsea frowned. "She likes you, but not me."

"That's not . . . I mean, why do you think so?"

"Because she asked *you* to go to the parade with her, that's why. And she *didn't* ask me!"

"Well," said Mary Lynne, "she probably just didn't think of it. You haven't been that friendly to her, anyway."

Then Mary Lynne began to chatter away about the party and how funny Thomas had looked with jello stuck to his face.

But Chelsea wasn't listening. Inside her was a horrible, heavy feeling. All week long she had suspected it, and now she knew it was true. Abigail MacCready, the new girl at school, was trying to steal Chelsea's best friend!

··3··

The Leprechaun Contest

At one o'clock on Sunday, an hour before the St. Patrick's Day parade was supposed to begin, Chelsea stood in a line of children waiting for the winner of the Leprechaun Contest to be announced.

"Hey," said a man holding a camera, "Nice costume!"

Chelsea grinned as he took her picture. "Thanks!"

All the trouble she'd gone to was worth it, she decided. She definitely looked like a leprechaun. But she wished the judges would hurry up!

Chelsea's mother stood close by. And way over

there was Mary Lynne, next to a sandy-haired woman.

That must be Mrs. MacCready, Chelsea thought. And the little boy in the stroller must be Abigail's brother.

At the other end of the leprechaun line stood Abigail. Her red hair poked out from under a tall silver-buckled hat. And she carried a pail filled with pretend treasure—gold-painted rocks.

Abigail looks good, all right. But still, my costume is better than hers, Chelsea told herself.

Chelsea was wearing a tall hat, too, and funny pointed shoes she'd made from construction paper. She had heavy fake eyebrows and fuzzy gray whiskers glued all around the edge of her face. But the best part was what she had done to her skin. It was green!

The idea had popped into her head just before it was time to leave for the contest. ''Just a minute, Mom,'' Chelsea had called as she ran upstairs to her room.

She snatched a green marker from her desk. Then she peered into her mirror and scribbled all over her forehead and nose and cheeks.

It looked good, she thought, it looked very good! So she covered her hands with green color, too— even her fingernails!

"Okay, I'm ready to go!" Chelsea skipped down the stairs.

Mrs. Martin stood in the hallway below, an astonished look on her face. "What have you done to yourself?" she cried.

Chelsea wondered why her mother seemed so worried. "You mean the green color? Don't you like it?"

"Well," said Mrs. Martin. She smiled weakly. "What if you stay green for the rest of your life?"

Silly Mom! thought Chelsea. "It's just marker," she explained. "After the contest, I'll wash it right off."

"We'll see." Mrs. Martin glanced at her watch. "We'd better get going."

Now the judges were pacing across the pavement, checking their clipboards and studying the contestants. Chelsea's chest felt tight with excitement.

I hope I win, she said to herself, I hope, I hope, I hope! If she did win, if she beat Abigail, then Mary Lynne would have to realize that *she*, not Abbie, was the person who would make the *best* best friend.

Oh!—Chelsea felt all shivery—the judges were ready to announce their decision!

She crossed her fingers and closed her eyes.

"And...the winner is...contestant number fifteen...Miss Chelsea Martin!"

Yaaay! I can't believe it! thought Chelsea. She jumped up and down, up and down, until she felt dizzy.

Her mother was excited, too. She had a big smile on her face as she came forward to hug Chelsea. The audience applauded and, Chelsea saw to her surprise, even Abigail was clapping for her.

A photographer from *The Sun* took Chelsea's picture while the judges shook her hand. Then a judge presented her with a fifty-dollar savings bond.

"We'll deposit that in your college fund," Mrs. Martin said.

Another judge handed Chelsea a tiny gift-wrapped box. She tore off the paper and lifted the lid. Inside, on a puffy piece of cotton, was a green enameled pin in the shape of a leprechaun.

"Oooh, that's pretty," said Mary Lynne as she peered over Chelsea's shoulder. "You deserved to win. Your costume is really good."

Chelsea grinned at her. "Thanks."

Later that afternoon, when the parade was over and Chelsea and her mother were home again, Chelsea called her father. Her parents were divorced, so Chelsea talked to her dad a lot on the phone and sometimes went for visits to Youngstown, Ohio, where he lived.

"Hello, Dad," she said. "Guess what? I won the Leprechaun Contest!"

"Wow!" said Mr. Martin. "Congratulations! I'm proud of you."

After they finished talking, Chelsea went upstairs to take a bath. Grass-colored skin was fine for a leprechaun, but now it was time to get back to normal.

Sitting in the tub, she took the bar of soap and rubbed it around and around between her palms. Gooshy green suds squished up through her fingers.

After washing herself all over, she sank down in the water to rinse off. It had been a good St. Patrick's Day parade, she thought.

She had especially enjoyed the bagpipe music. When the bagpipe band marched along the street, a small boy standing near Chelsea stuck his fingers in his ears. But Chelsea liked the strange sound. She liked the pipers' costumes, too—the plaid kilts and tall, furry hats.

And winning the contest—that was the most exciting thing that had ever happened to her! She couldn't wait to wear that pin to school tomorrow. Then *everyone* would know that she had had the best costume.

Chelsea rinsed herself off and stood up, ready to step out of the tub. But—wait a minute! She stared at her hands. Oh, no! They were still green—a paler green than before, but green just the same.

It was the shade of skin that she imagined an alien from outer space would have. But I'm not an alien, thought Chelsea, as she wrapped a towel around her shoulders. And I don't want to look like one!

Holding her fingers in front of her eyes as if she were watching a scary movie, she stood in front of the mirror. She took a deep breath and then peeked at her reflection. Her face was the color of little green apples.

I have to *do* something, Chelsea said to herself.

Perhaps she just needed to scrub harder. If she washed her hands and face really well, maybe the green stuff would come off.

Chelsea ran water into the sink, then squirted a glob of soft soap into her palm. She began to rub her hands together. She rubbed and rubbed, and rubbed some more.

But it was no use. Like a pair of gloves, the green color covered her fingers. Like a mask, it covered her face.

Maybe her mother was right—she would have to stay green the rest of her life!

What would that be like? Chelsea remembered seeing Kermit the Frog on television singing "It's Not Easy Being Green."

She pictured herself walking down the street, minding her own business. "Look everybody!"

someone would shout suddenly. "There she is—the green girl!" People would stop what they were doing and point and stare at her.

Chelsea sighed. At least she'd be famous.

There was a knock on the bathroom door. "Chelsea!" called Mrs. Martin. "You've been in there an awfully long time. Is everything all right?"

Chelsea looked around for a place to hide.

"Are you all right?" Mrs. Martin repeated.

Chelsea thought she might as well get it over with. Slowly, she opened the door.

Eyebrows raised, her mother stood looking at her. "I don't understand," she said. "Why didn't you wash your hands and face?"

Chelsea shifted from one foot to the other. "I *did* wash them."

Her mother's puzzled expression turned to a look of dismay. "You mean that green color didn't come off?"

Chelsea gazed down at her bare toes. "Uh-huh."

Mrs. Martin reached for a washcloth. "Maybe you didn't scrub hard enough." She wet the washcloth and began to rub Chelsea's face. Chelsea scrunched her eyes shut. Maybe the green color wasn't disappearing, but she felt as if her skin were starting to rub away!

"Oh, dear," Chelsea's mother said after a few minutes. She put down the washcloth. "You're right. This isn't working." She looked thoughtfully at Chelsea. "Show me the marker you used."

Chelsea went to her bedroom. In a few moments, she came back with a green felt-tipped pen.

"Uh-oh," said Mrs. Martin. "I was afraid of that. This is a permanent marker—it's waterproof."

Now Chelsea was really worried. If even her mother couldn't get rid of the green color, she was in big trouble!

Mrs. Martin sighed. "Well, I'm sure it will wear off in a day or two. But I don't see how you can go to school tomorrow looking like that."

Not go to school? Stay home? Oh, no! thought Chelsea—not tomorrow! There were lots of days she would love to stay home. But tomorrow she was going to show everyone her leprechaun pin.

"But Mo-om!" Chelsea wailed.

Mrs. Martin shook her head. "I'm afraid you'd be too much of a distraction. You look so... *strange*. Everyone would be watching you instead of paying attention to the teacher."

She patted Chelsea on the shoulder. "Don't worry—I'm sure you can stay with Mrs. DeCastro while I'm at work. Now it's time for bed."

Feeling very gloomy, Chelsea went to her bedroom. It's not fair, she thought, as she pulled her nightshirt over her head. It's not fair at all!

··4··

Green Is for Envy

"How do I look?" Chelsea asked when she met Mary Lynne at the corner Tuesday morning.

Mary Lynne stared at Chelsea. "You still look a *tiny* bit green. As if you're about to be carsick or something."

"That's what I thought," said Chelsea. "But I'm hoping nobody will notice."

On Monday, she had rubbed and scrubbed her face over and over—fifty times maybe. And she had washed her hands a hundred times at least! Finally, the green color had faded enough so that she didn't look too strange.

When she got to school, Chelsea hung her denim

jacket in her locker. Then she bent her chin so she could see the leprechaun pin that she'd fastened to the collar of her turtleneck shirt.

She couldn't wait to tell everyone about the St. Patrick's Day contest. But she didn't want to brag. She'd wait until one of her friends—Katie Klein, maybe, or Lucy Burnett—said, "What a cute pin! Where did you get that?"

"Thank you," Chelsea would answer, "I won it at the St. Patrick's Day contest on Sunday."

But to Chelsea's disappointment, no one said anything at all about the little green leprechaun. Until lunchtime, that is. Then Beverly Ann leaned across Paula and pointed at Chelsea's shirt. "Why are you wearing *that*? St. Patrick's Day is over!"

Chelsea smiled. At last! Someone had noticed her pin. "I won—" she began.

Paula interrupted. "Chelsea, do you feel all right? You look kind of funny."

"Yeah," said Lucy Burnett, who was sitting across the table. "You look kind of. . .green!"

Chelsea was embarrassed. She had wanted attention, but not this kind of attention. "It's just green marker that didn't all wash off," she said quickly. "But let me tell you about the con—"

"Marker!" said Beverly Ann. "You put marker all over your *face*?"

"Why did you do that?" asked Paula.

Chelsea was getting annoyed. "I'm trying to tell you!"

"Well, scribbling on yourself is an awfully babyish thing to do!" Beverly Ann said. Then she cupped her hands around her mouth and leaned across the table. She whispered something to Lucy Burnett, something that Chelsea couldn't quite hear.

Lucy's eyes widened. She turned her head to gaze along the lunch table.

What is Lucy looking at? thought Chelsea. There was nothing to see, except the other girls who were sitting at the table. Katie was next to Lucy, and then came Mary Lynne, who was sitting on Katie's other side, next to Abigail.

Beverly Ann glanced at Chelsea. Then, with a smirk on her face, she leaned forward to whisper again.

Chelsea felt her face turn red. Somehow she knew, she just *knew*, that Beverly Ann was talking about her!

She glared at Beverly Ann. "What did you say to Lucy?" she demanded. "Come on—I want to know!"

Beverly Ann tossed her head so that her long blonde hair swooshed back and forth. "Oh, nothing," she said.

Nothing! thought Chelsea. That's not true. I know she said something about me. And it had to be something bad!

Quietly, Paula turned to Chelsea. "I heard what Beverly Ann told Lucy," she whispered. "She said you turned green because you're jealous!"

Chelsea was confused. "What do you mean?"

"Well...," Paula hesitated. "She said it's because Mary Lynne is sitting next to Abbie instead of you. It's one of those sayings, you know—'turning green with envy.'"

"Oh!" Chelsea looked down at the lunch table.

"She was just kidding," said Paula. "I mean, even if you did think Mary Lynne liked Abigail better than you, you wouldn't turn green!'' Paula giggled. ''That's just silly.''

Chelsea didn't say anything. Of course she wasn't jealous! But was the other part true? *Did* Mary Lynne like Abigail better than she liked her?

That evening, just before dinner, Chelsea got a telephone call from her father. Chelsea told him about the new book her reading group had started on, *A Voyage to Different Lands.*

But in the middle of describing the first story, Chelsea found herself telling her father about Abigail, the new girl at school. ''Mary Lynne likes her,'' she said. ''Maybe even more than she likes me.''

''Really? But I know Mary Lynne likes you a lot,'' Mr. Martin assured her.

''She used to, anyway.'' Chelsea wound the telephone cord around her finger. ''But I'm not even sure if I'm still her best friend.''

There was a little silence, then Mr. Martin said, ''Why can't all three of you be friends? You and Mary Lynne and Abigail.''

''We can't, Daddy. Best friends are just two people.''

"Not always. What about my favorite characters—the Three Musketeers?"

"Who are they?"

"Three best friends," said Mr. Martin. "If you want to know more about them, look up the subject in your encyclopedia."

Oh! Chelsea hated it when her father told her to look up something. Why couldn't he just *tell* her?

Then she grinned. I know how to get back at him, she thought. "Oh, Dad, guess what we're having for dinner?"

"I don't know—what?"

"One of your favorites—eggplant parmigiana."

"Oh!" There was a pause, and Chelsea imagined her father wrinkling his nose. "That's nice," he said weakly.

Chelsea giggled. She knew he didn't really mean it. As much as her father loved pizza—and that was an awful lot—that's how much he hated eggplant!

"Well," said Chelsea, "I have to go now—dinner's ready. And I can't wait to eat that yummy eggplant!"

Mr. Martin laughed. "Okay, honey. Goodbye."

After dinner, Chelsea got out the "M" volume of her encyclopedia set. There wasn't much information about the Three Musketeers—just that they were characters in a book, and they were French.

But it also said that they were great friends, and their motto was "One for all, and all for one."

Three friends, thought Chelsea. That would be nice. But it would never, ever work for Mary Lynne and Abigail and me.

··5··

Family Fun Night

"Come on," said Mary Lynne at recess on Friday. "Let's find Abigail and jump rope."

"Do we *have* to?" said Chelsea. "I'm tired of jumping rope."

Mary Lynne frowned. "What do you mean? You've hardly jumped at all this week." She put her hands on her hips. "I think you just don't want to play with Abbie!"

Chelsea didn't know what to say. She didn't want to admit that Mary Lynne was right. "I don't think Abigail likes me very much," she mumbled at last.

"You keep saying that, but you know it's not true!" Mary Lynne said indignantly. "You're the one who doesn't like Abigail!''

Chelsea stared down at the scrubby playground grass and drew an imaginary circle with her toe. But I'm not the one who started it, she thought. I'm not trying to steal someone's best friend.

"You never talk to her," said Mary Lynne. "She thinks you're stuck-up."

What! Chelsea couldn't believe it. Me! she thought, stuck-up! Why, I'm the most unstuck-up person in the third grade...in the whole school ...probably, in the whole world!

"Don't get mad," said Mary Lynne. "Just come with me right now and talk to her. Then you'll find out how nice she is."

"Well...all right."

Abigail was sprawled across the jungle gym. As Chelsea and Mary Lynne approached, she hopped down and took a few steps toward them.

Show-off! thought Chelsea, when she noticed the jump rope that Abigail wore around her waist. She doesn't want anybody to forget how good she is at double-unders and all those other jump-rope tricks.

Now that Mary Lynne had dragged her over here, Chelsea was a little embarrassed. Her face felt stiff and strange, as if she were wearing a mask. She had to say something. "Uh...hello."

"Hello." Abigail didn't smile, either.

Chelsea stood awkwardly, staring off into space. What was she supposed to do now?

"It's Family Fun Night at school this evening," Mary Lynne said finally. "Are you two going?"

Chelsea nodded. "I am. My mother is working at the funnel-cake booth from six to seven."

Mary Lynne turned to Abigail. "How about you?"

"I'm not sure." Abigail wrinkled her forehead. "Is it really fun?"

"Sure," said Mary Lynne. "There's lots of games and food and stuff. And if they have goldfish again this year, I'm going to try to win one."

"What kinds of games?"

"Well, there's one where you can hook prizes with little fishing poles," said Mary Lynne, "and there's a grab bag..."

As Mary Lynne chattered away about Family

Fun Night, Chelsea could feel her mouth turning down. This isn't much fun, she thought. Mary Lynne is talking to Abigail, and she's forgotten all about me. I might as well be invisible.

Reaching into her pocket, she found a stubby piece of chalk. She crouched and began to draw a tic-tac-toe game on the blacktop.

Let's see, Chelsea said to herself, you're supposed to put X in the center square first. And O goes over there.

She looked up at Mary Lynne and Abigail. They were chattering away as if she—Chelsea—didn't even exist.

Angrily, she jumped to her feet. Jamming the piece of chalk into her pocket, she turned her back on the other girls and walked away. I hope, she thought, Abigail *doesn't* come to Family Fun Night!

As soon as Chelsea and her mother arrived at school that evening, Chelsea caught a glimpse of Mary Lynne in her favorite blue T-shirt. She was at the old fishing hole booth, holding a child-sized fishing rod that had a magnet on the end instead of a hook.

Chelsea started toward her. Then Mary Lynne shifted her position, and Chelsea had a brief view of red hair. Oh, no! thought Chelsea crossly. Abigail was standing at the old fishing hole, too.

With the fishing rod, Mary Lynne was trying to pick up a prize from the bottom of a plastic wading pool. She kept missing, apparently, because the two girls were shrieking with laughter.

Very funny, thought Chelsea. She turned in the opposite direction and stalked off through the crowd. She was in line at the candy booth, trying to decide whether to buy Pixy Stix or a small bag of Jolly Ranchers, when she caught a whiff of a mouth-watering odor.

Katie Klein and Lucy Burnett were right behind her. "Look what we bought from your mother!" said Katie, holding out her paper plate. On it sat a curlicue of fried dough that had been dusted with powdered sugar. "A funnel cake!"

"Mmmm, they're delicious!" said Lucy.

"They do smell good," said Chelsea. "I think

I'll get one, too." She went to find the funnel-cake booth.

She made her way down the hallway, zigging and zagging through the crowd. The PTA is going to make a lot of money tonight, she thought.

All at once, Chelsea felt a hand between her shoulder blades, pushing her forward a few steps. Indignantly, she turned around. Oh! I should have known, she said to herself. Behind her stood Arthur Wilmot.

Chelsea was annoyed. "What do *you* want?"

"I spent all my money," said Arthur. "Then I remembered—you still owe me fifty cents!"

"I do not!" said Chelsea. "I don't have to give that money back!"

Arthur glared at her. "Do too!"

"Do not!"

"Do—" Arthur began, and then stopped. His parents had suddenly appeared beside him.

"Arthur, we're leaving now."

"Aaaw." Arthur scowled. "I'm not ready!"

"Sorry," said Mrs. Wilmot, and she led her son away.

Thank goodness he's gone, thought Chelsea as she hurried down the hallway. As soon as I find Mom, I'm going to ask her to take me home, too. Family Fun Night is no fun at all.

Mrs. Martin was bending over an electric frying pan in a little room off the cafeteria. Her face was pink, and beads of sweat dotted her forehead.

"Oh, Chelsea." Using a funnel, Mrs. Martin dribbled thick, golden batter into the spitting oil. "What are you doing in here?"

"First I want a funnel cake, and then I want to go home!"

Mrs. Martin looked up from the electric frying pan. "Aren't you having a good time?"

"No, I'm not!"

Chelsea's mother pushed her hair off her forehead. "Well, I really have to stay until seven o'clock, Chelsea. These cakes are popular, and we're short-handed."

Chelsea sighed as she picked up a cake. "Okay—but we're leaving right at seven. Promise!"

Her mother nodded. She was already busy with her spatula, lifting a golden-brown spiral of dough onto a paper towel to cool.

Nibbling at her funnel cake, Chelsea walked along the hallway. She studied the booths that lined the walls on both sides.

Maybe I'll buy one of those little stuffed animals, she thought. Just then, she heard Mary Lynne calling. "Hey Chelsea, wait up!"

Mary Lynne squeezed through the crowds of people. When she finally reached Chelsea, she stopped and tilted her head back like a baby bird. Then she held up a long, pencil-shaped tube of paper and shook a stream of candy granules into her mouth.

"I didn't know you were here!" she said after she swallowed. "Come and watch me win a goldfish!"

Chelsea hesitated, then smiled. "Okay." She let Mary Lynne pull her to the gymnasium where most of the games were grouped together.

There was a large crowd waiting for a turn at the goldfish booth. Chelsea groaned inside when she saw that the very first person in line was. . . Abigail.

Katie Klein's mother was in charge of the booth.

Abigail handed her a quarter and in return received three Ping-Pong balls.

She was supposed to toss them one at a time into the goldfish bowls that were set up on the floor. If she threw a ball into a bowl, she would win a goldfish.

Abigail aimed, then flicked the little white ball toward the center bowl. It circled the rim and then fell—plunk!—into the glass container.

"Yaaay!" Mary Lynne clapped her hands.

Chelsea frowned. Wouldn't you know it? Abigail, the champion rope jumper and soccer player, was an expert at tossing Ping-Pong balls as well.

Mrs. Klein handed Abigail a plastic bag that was half full of water. Inside, a yellow goldfish shimmered in the bright lights of the gymnasium.

"Look what I won!" Abigail said.

Mary Lynne squealed, "Oh, it's so cute!"

Chelsea peered at the goldfish. She had never thought of fish as being cute, exactly. They were so wet! Wet and slippery.

"You can pet him." Abigail set the plastic bag

on the floor and opened it. She stuck a finger into the water and delicately nudged the goldfish. Immediately, the fish flipped its tail and darted away.

"He doesn't like that," said Chelsea.

"Yes, he does."

Chelsea frowned. "No, he doesn't. Dogs like to be petted, not fish."

Abigail looked at her coldly. "How do *you* know?"

Mary Lynne glanced from Abigail to Chelsea. "It doesn't matter!"

Abigail shrugged. "You're right. Anyway, I think I have to go now. I see my parents over there with my little brother."

She tied a loose knot in the top of the bag and then handed it to Mary Lynne. "Here, you can have this fish. I don't really want it."

"I can?" Mary Lynne looked delighted. "That's great! I always have trouble getting those Ping-Pong balls to go in the right place, anyway."

Abigail started to leave, and Mary Lynne walked a few paces with her.

Hey, wait a minute! Chelsea thought as she

watched them say goodbye. Mary Lynne is *my* best friend! If anyone is going to give Mary Lynne a goldfish, it should be me!

Chelsea glanced at the line. By now, there were only two people—first graders—ahead of her. "I'll win a goldfish for you, too," Chelsea told Mary Lynne when she returned. "A silver one!"

Mary Lynne's big, brown eyes widened. "But Chelsea, I'm not sure my parents will let me take home more than one fish!"

Chelsea didn't listen. She was already digging in her pocket for a quarter. She had reached the front of the line, and she was determined to win a goldfish. If Abigail could do it, so could she!

··6··

Goldfish Fever

Smiling, Katie's mother took Chelsea's quarter and then handed her the Ping-Pong balls. But Chelsea didn't smile back. Winning a goldfish was much too serious to smile about!

She ran her thumb over the smooth, round ball. She rolled the ball between her fingertips. Then she closed her eyes and sent a mental message. *Okay, Ball, I want you to dive straight into one of those fishbowls.*

She took a deep breath. She swung her arm back. And then she let go. *In,* commanded Chelsea silently. Go in, go *in*!

The ball did go in—right into the center bowl. Chelsea blinked and stared; the Ping-Pong ball had followed her orders!

Hey! she said to herself, maybe I'm actually *good* at throwing balls into goldfish bowls.

"Very nice," said Mrs. Klein. "You win a fish."

Most of the goldfish looked as though they were really made of gold. But Chelsea pointed to one that was a gleaming silver color. "Could I have that one, please?"

A few seconds later Chelsea handed the fish to Mary Lynne. "Here you are."

"Oh. Thanks, Chelsea."

Chelsea grinned. "It was easy. Do you want another one?"

Mary Lynne hesitated. She looked down at the goldfish bags she was holding. "We-e-ll, I don't know, Chelsea..."

But Chelsea was already in line again. A few minutes later, when it was her turn, she took the Ping-Pong ball between her palms and held it up to her mouth. "Go in!" she whispered.

And the ball went in. She won another fish! She

ran around the waiting group of children and got in line again.

Half an hour later, Chelsea was just starting her fifth turn. She'd been concentrating so hard on winning that she hadn't even stopped to talk to Mary Lynne. But Chelsea was sure Mary Lynne was going to love all those fish.

She paused to push her sweaty hair off her forehead. It was hot here in the gymnasium, but she didn't want to quit now, not when she was doing so well.

Beverly Ann's mother had come to help Mrs. Klein with the goldfish booth. She looked doubtful as Chelsea held out a quarter.

''Are you sure you want another turn?'' she said as she handed Chelsea three more balls. ''Don't you have enough fish?''

''Uh...'' Chelsea glanced down. Clustered around her feet were six...seven...eight plastic bags. In each bag was a goldfish.

I guess I do have enough, thought Chelsea. I'll just throw these last three balls, and then I'll quit.

Ping! ping! ping! went the balls. Chelsea hadn't

tried especially hard—she threw one ball too far, and it flew out of the booth. But still she won two more fish.

"You can't carry all these plastic bags," said Beverly Ann's mother. "I'd better get a box."

She found a cardboard carton at the back of the booth. "There!" she said, piling the plastic bags into the box. "Are you sure you can handle this yourself?"

"Uh-huh," said Chelsea, although the box *was* pretty heavy. She glanced at the large clock on the wall of the gymnasium. It was almost seven. She had to get going. She had to find Mary Lynne, give her the goldfish, and then meet her mother in the lobby.

Where was Mary Lynne, anyway? Chelsea thought she'd be waiting right beside the goldfish booth. But there was no sign of her anywhere.

Chelsea looked around anxiously. I'd better go find her, she thought. But I'll have to hurry—I'm supposed to meet Mom in five minutes.

Chelsea scanned the crowd. A girl wearing a blue T-shirt was just walking out the door. "Mary

Lynne! Mary Lynne!" Chelsea shouted. Burdened by the heavy box of goldfish, she staggered across the gymnasium.

But when she reached the big double doors she could see that the person she'd been following wasn't Mary Lynne, after all.

She wasn't in the hallway, either. Chelsea headed for the lobby, checking all the booths along the way. Still, there was no sign of Mary Lynne.

By now Chelsea was worried and tired. The cardboard box was heavy!

Just then Katie Klein walked by. "Have you seen Mary Lynne?" asked Chelsea.

Katie nodded. "Yes, she went home a while ago."

Chelsea stared at Katie. "Are you sure? I have to give her these goldfish!"

Katie shrugged. "All I know is I saw her walk out the door with her parents."

Now what am I going to do? thought Chelsea. Then she heard a familiar voice.

"There you are," said Mrs. Martin. "Are you ready to leave?" She started for the front door, then stopped and looked back over her shoulder. "Chelsea, are you coming? What's in that box?"

"Uh..."

Chelsea's mother came closer. She peered into the cardboard carton, and her eyebrows went up. "Chelsea, there are one, two, three...ten goldfish here!"

"Don't worry!" Chelsea said quickly. "They're not *my* goldfish."

Mrs. Martin frowned. "Whose are they, then?"

"Well, I won them at the goldfish booth. But I told Mary Lynne they were for her."

"Oh, dear," said Chelsea's mother with a sigh. "Were Mary Lynne's parents with her? Did they agree that she could have all these fish?"

"Uh...no-o-o. Her parents weren't there. But you'll see, Mom, it'll be all right. I'll call Mary Lynne tomorrow morning, and she'll come and pick them up."

"Hmmm." Mrs. Martin looked doubtful. "Are you sure?"

Chelsea nodded. "Sure, I'm sure." But behind her back, Chelsea's fingers were crossed.

··7··

Poor Skippy!

It was Saturday morning, and Chelsea had just finished talking on the telephone to Mary Lynne.

"What time are the Woodlies coming to pick up the goldfish?" asked Mrs. Martin. She shook some fish flakes into the microwave cake pan they were using as a fishbowl.

Chelsea bent to tie her shoe. "Theyaren't goingtopickupthefish," she mumbled.

"What did you say, Chelsea? I didn't hear you."

Reluctantly, Chelsea stood and faced her mother. "You're not going to like it."

Mrs. Martin stared at Chelsea. "You mean..."

Chelsea nodded. "Mary Lynne can come over and play after lunch, but she *can't* take the fish home with her. Her parents said she could only have two goldfish—that's all.''

With a thump, Chelsea's mother sat down on a kitchen chair. ''You should've checked with me before playing that Ping-Pong game,'' she said in a grumpy voice. ''What are we going to do with all these fish?''

Chelsea felt guilty. She knew it was true—ten fish were too many. But it had been so much fun to win them! Once she had gotten started, she hadn't been able to stop. It was like eating potato chips.

Chelsea's mother got up and leaned over the kitchen counter to study the cake pan. ''Right now, the water needs to be changed.''

''Already?''

Mrs. Martin nodded. ''With ten fish in a bowl, the water gets dirty pretty quickly. You can do that, Chelsea. I need to run the vacuum.''

''Okay.''

Chelsea used a soup ladle to dip the fish out of the cake pan and into a mixing bowl filled with tap water. These fish are a lot of work, she thought, as she scooped them out, one by one.

As Chelsea carried the pan to the sink to empty it, she stared at the cloudy water. What were those little bits of stuff floating in it? Oh! Those specks were...were fish poop! That's how the water got dirty—the fish went to the bathroom right in their bowl!

Yuck! Chelsea decided to dump the dirty water into the toilet instead of the sink. And I'll have to remember never to eat any cake made in that micro-wave pan, she told herself afterwards.

At one o'clock, there was a knock at the front door. Chelsea opened it and found Mary Lynne standing there.

"Hi!" said Mary Lynne.

"Hi," said Chelsea. "Come on, let's get some cookies and go up to my room."

They went into the kitchen. Chelsea climbed on a chair and reached into the cupboard for a bag of Oreos.

"What's tha-at?" said Mary Lynne. She stood still like a statue and pointed to something lying on the shiny vinyl floor.

Chelsea climbed down to look. "Oh, no—

it's one of my fish. And it must be dead!"

"What happened?" asked Mary Lynne.

Chelsea inspected the microwave cake pan. "I think I know." She pointed to the fish lying on the floor. "That's Skippy. Last night he kept leaping up and skipping over the water."

Mary Lynne's eyes got big. "You mean, he jumped too far—right out of the pan?"

Chelsea sighed. "Uh-huh. It must have happened this morning some time."

"Oh, poor Skippy, poor little fish," said Mary Lynne. She squatted and poked with one finger at the dry fish corpse. "Uh...Chelsea?"

"What?"

"Let's have a funeral!"

"Ooooh," said Chelsea. "Yeah!" She picked up the fish with her fingertips, and they went upstairs to her room.

Tenderly, Chelsea laid Skippy in his coffin. Well, it wasn't exactly a coffin. It was the small cardboard box that her leprechaun pin had come in. It was just the right size for a goldfish.

Inside the box were two pieces of fuzzy white

cotton. Chelsea fixed the top layer of fluff so that it came up to the fish's chin, just like a blanket.

Mary Lynne set the lid on top of the box. "Okay," she said, "let's bury him!"

"Not yet." Chelsea got a pencil out of her desk. "We have to write an epi..." Chelsea couldn't remember the word she wanted. "An epi something...you know, words carved on a tombstone, like, 'Here lies Mary Smith, loving wife and mother—'"

"Oh, I get it!" said Mary Lynne. "How about this epi? 'Here lies Skippy, loving father—'"

"No." Chelsea shook her head. "We don't even know if he was married!"

"Then, 'Here lies Skippy, a good fish.' How about that?"

"Hmmm, it's sort of short."

Mary Lynne stared thoughtfully into space. "I know!" she said after a few seconds.

"Here lies a fish;
His name was Skippy.
He jumped too far,
And now he's history!"

"No, no, no!" said Chelsea. "That makes it sound like it was his fault he died."

Mary Lynne shrugged. "It *was* his fault."

"Not really," said Chelsea. "I guess we should have put the fish in a deeper container. Then Skippy wouldn't have been able to jump all the way out of the bowl."

"Oh. Okay. . . how about this:

Here lies Skippy the fish,
Who Chelsea put in a flat dish.
He suddenly jumped out,"

Mary Lynne hesitated. "And. . .and. . . Now Chelsea does nothing but pout!"

Chelsea frowned. "I don't like that, either."

"Okay, then you think of something."

"All right. Just a minute." Chelsea began doodling on a sheet of paper.

"Okay," she said, after a few moments. "The title is 'Skippy.' And it goes like this:

The finest fish in all the land,
He lived in a microwave cake pan.
It wasn't his fault he jumped too far.
Now he's gone to live upon a star!

"There!" said Chelsea proudly.

"We-ell," said Mary Lynne, "do you really think he's living on a star? *I* don't."

"No...probably not. But that doesn't matter. It's just supposed to sound good."

"Okay," said Mary Lynne. "It's your fish. Write it down, and then we can get to the good part. Uh-oh!"

"What?" Chelsea had already printed a few tiny letters on the box lid. She looked up and saw Mary Lynne pointing toward the bedroom window.

"It's raining. We can't bury him now!"

"Oh, darn!" Chelsea was disappointed. But maybe, she thought, there was something else they could do. "What about a funeral like they have in India? You know, where they put the body up on a platform and then set it on fire?"

Mary Lynne stared at Chelsea. "We can't do that! Probably, the curtains would burst into flames and we'd have to call 9-1-1 and the fire truck would come and they'd have to break all the windows to let out the smoke and—"

Chelsea put up her hand to stop the flow of

words. "Well, what if we put Skippy in a frying pan on the stove and get my mother to turn on the burner?"

Mary Lynne shook her head. "That wouldn't be a funeral, Chelsea. That would be fried fish!"

Chelsea frowned. Mary Lynne didn't understand at all. But maybe the frying pan idea wasn't very good.

A new thought popped into Chelsea's head. "I know! We'll have a burial at sea!"

Mary Lynne looked puzzled. "How can we do that?"

"We'll use the bathroom," said Chelsea. "My mom puts Tidy Bowl in the toilet, so there's even blue water!"

"Okay." Mary Lynne nodded. "A burial at sea makes sense—Skippy *is* a fish."

The two girls ran to the bathroom. They positioned themselves on either side of the toilet and lifted the seat cover.

Chelsea stared down at the ultramarine blue water. She imagined that she and Mary Lynne were in a boat, far out at sea. After all, that's where the toilet water would end up eventually, wouldn't it? In the ocean?

She lifted the lid off the cardboard box and pulled back the top layer of cotton. Carefully, she picked up Skippy by the tail.

"Oka-a-ay, I'll just say a few farewell words, and then I'll drop him in." Chelsea held the fish above the toilet.

"Goodbye, Skippy," she pronounced solemnly. "You were a good fish while you lasted—"

Mary Lynne interrupted. "I want to say something, too. A prayer."

Chelsea sighed. "Oh, all right."

"Okay, close your eyes. Are you ready?"

"Yes."

"God is great, God is good. And we thank him for our—"

Chelsea opened her eyes. "Stop! You can't use that prayer—that's something people say before dinner. We're not going to eat Skippy!"

"Oh." Mary Lynne nibbled on her bottom lip. "How about 'Now I Lay Me Down to Sleep'?"

Chelsea considered it. "Okay," she said.

Mary Lynne went ahead with the prayer, and Chelsea got ready to drop the goldfish into the toilet. "One...two...three!"

"Bombs away!" yelled Mary Lynne.

Bombs away? thought Chelsea. That didn't seem right. But she opened her fingers and released Skippy's tail. Skippy plunged into the water with a little splash.

Mary Lynne reached to flush the toilet.

"No!" said Chelsea. "I want to do it—he's my fish." Thump! She pressed on the handle.

Swish...gurgle, gurgle, gurgle!

The blue water turned into a whirlpool that disappeared down the hole. And along with the water went Skippy.

"Goodbye, Skippy," said Chelsea. "Goodbye!"

··8··

Thomas Spills the Beans

On the way to school Monday morning, all Mary Lynne wanted to talk about was fish. "I named my goldfish Lucy and Desi," she said. "They're so-o-o cute! I'm keeping them in a bowl on my nightstand so I can see them as soon as I wake up."

"That's nice," said Chelsea politely.

"Did you name the rest of your fish?" asked Mary Lynne.

"No," Chelsea admitted. To tell the truth, she was tired of goldfish.

They were awfully messy, for one thing. She had to change their water every day. And she couldn't do anything with them—couldn't take them for walks or cuddle them in her lap. All she could do, really, was look at them. For Chelsea, that wasn't enough.

"That funeral we had Saturday was fun," Mary Lynne went on. "Except, I guess it wasn't fun for Skippy."

"Yeah, poor Skippy." Chelsea tried to arrange her face in a mournful expression.

But Mary Lynne was right—the funeral had been fun. And the best part was that Chelsea had been alone with Mary Lynne, without Abigail hanging around.

When the girls arrived at school, Chelsea spotted Abigail's red hair right away. With her jump rope tucked under one arm, Abigail waited for them at the edge of the playground.

Mary Lynne waved. "Hi, Abbie!"

Chelsea didn't wave. Oh, groan! she said to herself. It's *her* again. But when Mary Lynne started off in Abigail's direction, Chelsea reluctantly followed.

Just as the girls reached the playground, one of

the third-grade boys—Thomas—came pounding toward them. "Hey, Chelsea! Hey, Mary Lynne!" he yelled.

Chelsea stared. What does he want? she wondered.

Thomas sat down on the blacktop, untied his shoe, and took it off.

"What are you doing?" asked Mary Lynne.

"I'm just getting out my money," said Thomas as he pulled off his white tube sock.

Now Abigail spoke up. "Your money? What for?"

"So I can pay Mary Lynne and Chelsea. I want them to do a job for me."

Uh-oh! Immediately, Chelsea began to worry. She didn't know what Thomas had in mind, but she hoped this job business didn't have anything to do with Arthur Wilmot. After all, Thomas was Arthur's best friend.

Mary Lynne seemed puzzled. "A job?" she said. "What do you mean?"

Thomas put down his sock. He reached into his pocket, pulled out a crumpled sheet of pink construction paper, and held it up. The paper was exactly like the one Arthur had been carrying around last week.

"Oh, I'd almost forgotten about that!" said Mary Lynne. "It's one of the ads we made, Chelsea."

"I know," Chelsea said glumly.

Thomas waved the pink paper at Mary Lynne. "Like it says in your ad," he explained. "I want *you* to do something that *I* don't want to do."

"What?"

"My math homework. I guess I watched too much TV last night 'cause I didn't have time to do it."

Chelsea stared at Thomas. Was he serious? He expected them to do his homework?

Mary Lynne put one hand on her hip. "Huh?"

"What is he talking about?" said Abigail.

Beverly Ann was standing nearby. "Yeah," she said. "What are you talking about?"

"Butt out, you two." Thomas frowned at Beverly Ann and Abigail. "My business is with Mary Lynne and Chelsea."

Thomas took his arithmetic book out of his backpack. "It was page eighty-five, remember? One through twenty. How about if Mary Lynne does the odd problems and Chelsea does the evens?"

Chelsea shook her head.

"You're crazy!" snapped Mary Lynne.

Thomas shrugged. "Okay, divide it up any way you want, as long as it's finished before math period." Thomas held his sock upside down, and two shiny dimes fell out onto the blacktop. "And I'll pay you, of course."

He stood and held out the dimes. "Here, one for each of you."

"A measly dime apiece!" said Mary Lynne. "You must be kidding!"

Thomas was indignant. "Your ad said you worked cheap!"

Mary Lynne tossed her head. "Not *that* cheap!"

"Besides," said Chelsea, "doing homework for somebody else would be cheating!"

"Oh yeah?" Thomas scowled. He turned to Chelsea. "Well, you're a cheater anyway!"

"What do you mean? I am not!"

"Yes, you are! You messed up that job for Arthur, and then you wouldn't give his money back!"

Chelsea glared at Thomas. "Oh, go away!"

Keep quiet, Mr. Blabbermouth—that's what she felt like saying. She glanced uneasily at the other girls.

What would Abigail do, wondered Chelsea, if she found out that Arthur had wanted to be her boyfriend? And what if she found out that Chelsea had told him she'd said no?

I have to do something quick, Chelsea decided, before Thomas spills the beans. That's what her father called it when someone told a secret—"spilling the beans."

Maybe she could change the subject. "Uh. . .it's getting late—let's go jump rope before the bell rings."

"All right," said Abigail. She took her jump rope from under her arm.

But Mary Lynne didn't budge. "Wait a minute!" She turned to Thomas. "What are you talking about? We never did a job for Arthur.''

"That's not true—Chelsea did!''

Chelsea felt everyone's eyes on her. Something terrible was about to happen—she just knew it.

Mary Lynne looked at her curiously. "Is that right, Chelsea? Did Arthur give you a job to do?''

"I forget,'' Chelsea said.

"I don't like to be called a liar!'' Thomas said. "You *did* do something for Arthur—remember? He asked you to...'' Thomas seemed embarrassed. "To find out...you know, about Abigail.''

Abigail raised her eyebrows. "Me? What are you talking about?''

"You know. Arthur wanted you to be his girlfriend.''

"What!''

Thomas seemed puzzled. "Don't you remember? Arthur gave Chelsea fifty cents to ask you to be his girlfriend. Like those Pilgrims, John Alden and Priscilla what's-her-name.''

Abigail turned to Chelsea. "You never told me!''

All the girls were looking at Chelsea now, giving her cold stares of disapproval. Chelsea

looked down at her shoes. She didn't say anything. What *could* she say?

"I can't believe you did that!" Beverly Ann
declared.

"Me, neither!" said Mary Lynne.

"You never told me Arthur wanted me to be his
girlfriend," Abigail repeated. "I think you're
mean!" She stomped off across the playground.
Beverly Ann followed, and Mary Lynne hurried
after them, stopping just once to glance over her
shoulder at Chelsea.

Thomas stared at Chelsea. "I don't get it. You
mean you *didn't* do the job for Arthur?"

"Well...," said Chelsea uncomfortably,
"not exactly."

Thomas stuck his arithmetic book back in his
backpack. He shrugged; then he wandered off,
shaking his head in disgust.

Glumly, Chelsea gazed at the disappearing backs
of her classmates. Why do these things always
happen to me? she wondered. I probably don't
have a single friend left in third grade!

··9··

A Surprise for Mrs. DeCastro

When Mrs. Martin got home from work that day, she looked at Chelsea and said, "What's wrong, honey?"

"Oh, nothing." Chelsea didn't want to tell her mother the truth—that all her friends hated her.

Her mother might say that it was Chelsea's fault. She might say that Chelsea had gotten herself into this mess, and now there was nothing to do except tell Abigail she was sorry.

I *am* sorry, Chelsea thought. But just thinking about apologizing made her poke out her lower lip. Maybe she had told a little fib. But nobody's perfect, especially not that best-friend-stealing Abigail!

Chelsea's mother still seemed worried. "Are you

sure nothing's wrong?'' she asked, as she made a cup of decaf coffee. "You look like something's wrong."

Chelsea flopped into a chair. "I'm sure." She stretched her mouth wide. "See, I'm smiling."

"Well...all right." Mrs. Martin glanced at the cake-pan fishbowl on the counter. "Oh, dear," she said with a sigh, "the fish need clean water again."

Chelsea felt guilty. She hopped up from her chair. "Don't worry—I'll do it. You go sit down."

Mrs. Martin smiled. "Okay, thanks Chelsea." She headed for the living room to read the evening newspaper.

Chelsea dumped out the dirty water. Then she decided she was going to find a different bowl for the goldfish.

They didn't have a real glass fishbowl. But at least, Chelsea thought, I could put the fish into a deeper container. Then there wouldn't be any more fish bodies on the floor.

Chelsea opened a kitchen cupboard. On the second shelf were plastic bowls, measuring cups, and two tall, navy blue, plastic juice pitchers.

One of them would make a perfect fishbowl—nice and deep. Except it was too bad you couldn't see through it, the way you could through a regular fishbowl.

Chelsea stood on a chair and took a pitcher from the cupboard. She held it under the tap until it was half-full of water.

There! she told herself after putting all the goldfish inside. No fish can jump out of that! She sprinkled in some food flakes, stuck the lid on the pitcher, and flipped up the spout cap so the fish would have air. Then she set the pitcher on the kitchen counter beside the toaster.

After dinner, Chelsea's mother picked up a stack of newspapers from the coffee table and carried them into the kitchen. She ran a dustcloth over the living room tables. Then she began to vacuum the carpet.

"Why are you cleaning?" asked Chelsea. Her mother usually did her housework on the weekends.

"Oh, didn't I tell you? The neighborhood association is having a meeting this evening." Mrs. Martin sighed. "It's my turn to be hostess."

"Can I help?" said Chelsea. "There's no school tomorrow, remember? It's a teachers' workshop day."

Chelsea's mother considered. "Yes, I guess you can stay up late."

"Yaaay!" said Chelsea.

Mrs. Martin surveyed the living room. "Hmmm, this place looks pretty good...except, Chelsea, would you please take your Monopoly game up to your bedroom?"

"Sure, Mom."

When she came downstairs again, Chelsea helped arrange Oreos and chocolate chip cookies on a gold-edged serving plate. Her mother had the coffee brewing, and she was setting out cream and sugar.

Everything was ready, and just in time—the doorbell was ringing. Already, the first person had arrived.

Soon the living room was full of people. They smiled and talked, exchanging tidbits of news. "What a big girl you are now, Chelsea!" somebody exclaimed. "What grade are you in this year?"

asked someone else.

One or two people even tried to pat her on the head. But Chelsea ducked out of reach just in time.

After the meeting was called to order, Chelsea got out her colored pencils. She sat on the floor and drew pictures while the grownups talked.

Forty-five minutes later, the business part of the meeting was over. It was time for refreshments. Chelsea passed around the plate of cookies while her mother served cups of coffee.

"We have iced tea, also," said Mrs. Martin. "At least—" A crease appeared between her eyebrows.

"Oh, dear, I guess I forgot to make it. Chelsea, could you possibly do it? I think the pitcher's already on the counter. And the tea mix is there, too."

Chelsea went into the kitchen. A canister of instant tea and a dark blue pitcher were beside the toaster. Chelsea hesitated. Her mother said the pitcher for the iced tea was on the counter. But—

Just then, Mrs. Martin hurried into the kitchen. "Chelsea, I told Mrs. Reeder about the play you wrote last Thanksgiving, and she'd like to look at it. She's a retired English teacher, you know."

"Why does she want to see my play?" asked Chelsea. "She's not going to grade it, is she?"

"No, of course not; she's just interested. Would you run up to your room and get it, please?"

"But what about the tea?"

"Don't worry," said Mrs. Martin. "I'll finish up. It'll just take me a minute to get out the ice."

When Chelsea came downstairs, her mother was setting a blue pitcher and a tray of tall metal tumblers on the coffee table. "Oh, there you are, Chelsea," said Mrs. Martin. "Would you help our guests with the iced tea while I show your play to Mrs. Reeder?"

Chelsea was holding a bundle of looseleaf pages stuck together with a paper clip. She handed the pages to her mother and then went over to the coffee table.

The Martins' next-door neighbor, Mrs. DeCastro, sat on the sofa nearby. "Would you like iced tea, Mrs. DeCastro?" asked Chelsea.

Mrs. DeCastro smiled. "I'd love some." Chelsea handed her a blue metal tumbler and a napkin.

"Thank you, Chelsea," Mrs. DeCastro said.

"You're welcome."

"Maybe I'd better pour." Mrs. DeCastro reached for the pitcher. "It was so nice of your mother to have everyone here this evening."

"Uh-huh." Chelsea took an Oreo cookie from the plate on the coffee table.

Mrs. DeCastro went on. "It's so. . .EEEK!"

Chelsea had taken her cookie apart and was licking the filling from one half. She stared at her next-door neighbor. What was going on?

Mrs. DeCastro was looking into her metal tumbler. Her face was pale. There was a wet spot on her slacks where some liquid had sloshed onto her lap.

"What is it?" called Chelsea's mother from across the room. "What's wrong?"

"Look!" Mrs. DeCastro held out her glass.

Mrs. Martin came closer. She stared down into the blue tumbler; then her eyes got big and round. "What on earth?"

Chelsea's stomach felt queasy. She had a feeling that—somehow!—she was in trouble.

"Chelsea!" said Mrs. Martin.

Chelsea jumped.

"Come here and look."

Chelsea peered into Mrs. DeCastro's tea glass. Oh, *no*! Flipping their tails and swishing round and round among the ice cubes were one...two... three goldfish!

"Is this a practical joke, Chelsea?" asked Mrs. Martin.

Chelsea was so astonished she couldn't speak. She just shook her head.

Then Mrs. Martin turned to her neighbor. "I'm awfully sorry, Nancy! I can't imagine how—"

Mrs. DeCastro laughed. "Oh, it's all right. Those goldfish just startled me, that's all. Just think!—I almost swallowed them!"

Everyone came over to look into Mrs. DeCastro's glass. No one had ever served goldfish at a neighborhood meeting before.

"I want to find out exactly what happened, Chelsea," Mrs. Martin said. "How did those goldfish get into the pitcher?"

"I put them in there before dinner," Chelsea

said. "I didn't want any more fish to jump out of that cake pan and die." She looked down at her toes. "I guess I should have told you."

"I didn't even notice the cake pan was gone. But what happened to the tea you made?"

"I didn't get a chance to make it. You asked me to go upstairs and get my play to show Mrs. Reeder."

"Oh. Well, then it was my fault, too," said Mrs. Martin. "I was in a hurry. The pitcher felt heavy, and I just assumed it was full of tea."

"And I thought you made tea in the *other* pitcher," said Chelsea.

"I'm going to make some right now," her mother said.

"I'll help," said Mrs. DeCastro as she followed Mrs. Martin into the kitchen.

Chelsea wanted to help, too, so she passed around the plate of cookies again. When everyone had finished eating refreshments and discussing the latest news, the neighbors went home.

Chelsea and her mother waved goodbye to Mrs. DeCastro.

"Thanks again," she said with a laugh. "I

won't forget my delicious goldfish tea!''

Mrs. Martin piled dirty cups and saucers into the dishwasher. ''I've been thinking, Chelsea. Maybe these pet fish aren't working out very well for us.''

Chelsea sighed. ''I know. Do you think we can give them away?''

''We can try. Maybe there are people right here in our neighborhood who would love to have a goldfish.''

''Uh-huh.'' Then Chelsea muttered, ''I'm sorry I spoiled your meeting.''

''Oh, I don't think you spoiled anything.'' Mrs. Martin smiled. ''I have a feeling that was one neighborhood get-together that people will be talking about for a long time!''

··10··

The Great Goldfish Giveaway

After breakfast the next day, Mrs. Martin got out the empty jars and bottles she'd been saving to take to the recycling center. They would make good goldfish containers.

Chelsea went to look for her big red wagon. She hadn't played with it for a while, but it would be perfect for hauling goldfish from house to house.

"This is the last one," Chelsea's mother said, as she found space in the wagon for a fish in a pickle jar. "Now remember, only go to the houses of people we know."

"I'm just going down this block and the next," said Chelsea. "Don't worry."

Mrs. DeCastro's house was right next door, so Chelsea decided to start with her. She stood on tiptoes and lifted the brass door knocker. Bang! Bang! Bang!

In just a few seconds, Mrs. DeCastro opened the door.

Chelsea tried to imagine what the announcer on the home shopping channel would say. "Hello, Mrs. DeCastro," she said. "I have a very good offer today. I'm giving away goldfish, absolutely free."

Mrs. DeCastro hesitated. "Well, I really don't *want* a goldfish, especially after what happened last night. But I'll take one, as a favor to your mother."

"Oh, great!" Chelsea was delighted. Now, she had only eight more fish to give away.

She had good luck at the next house and the next one after that. By the time she had reached the end of the block, she had only four fish left! And she gave away two more to Mrs. Reeder, who lived in the green-shuttered house on the corner.

"I'm almost finished reading your play," Mrs. Reeder said. "It's good; I like it a lot."

Chelsea smiled. "Thanks."

Confidently, she pulled her wagon along the sidewalk. Only two more fish to go! she thought as she started down the next block.

But there she wasn't so lucky. After knocking at five houses, she still had two goldfish. She visited five more houses, but only one person was home. He told Chelsea he was certain he didn't want a goldfish. The two jars stayed in her wagon.

Up ahead was the last house on the block. But that was the house where Thomas lived! She wasn't going to knock on *his* door. I'll just have to take the last two fish home again, she thought.

Chelsea bumped the old red wagon across a crack in the sidewalk. The goldfish jars clanged together, but Chelsea didn't care. She was tired of knocking on doors; she wanted to go home.

"Hey!" someone yelled. "Hey, Chelsea-Delsea!"

Chelsea glanced over her shoulder. Oh, no! It was Arthur—of all people!—coming out of Thomas's house. Down the driveway he strolled, with his hands in his pockets.

Chelsea bent her head and kept going. She

walked fast. Clink! clank! clink! went the goldfish jars. Slap, slap, slap came the sound of Arthur's shoes on the sidewalk.

All of a sudden, he was standing in front of her, blocking the way. Before he even opened his mouth, Chelsea knew what he was going to say.

"Hey, Chelsea, when're you going to give my two quarters back?"

Oooh! thought Chelsea. When is Arthur going to stop complaining about that fifty cents!

"And that's not all!" Arthur said. "Thomas told me that you lied! You never asked Abigail if she'd be my girlfriend!"

"So what?" said Chelsea. "You could ask her yourself."

Arthur shrugged. "Naaww, I changed my mind about having a girlfriend. But I still want my fifty—"

Chelsea refused to listen. She covered her ears.

Arthur frowned. He crossed his arms on his chest and talked very loud indeed! Now, even with her hands over her ears, she could hear him plainly.

Chelsea wished Arthur would go away! If I

had fifty cents with me, she thought, I'd hand it over just to get rid of him.

Hmmm. Chelsea glanced down at the red wagon. She didn't have fifty cents, but she did have two goldfish.

"You'd just better give my money back!" Arthur shouted. "I—"

Chelsea interrupted. "Be quiet, Arthur, and let me talk!"

"Huh?" Arthur glared at Chelsea. "Oh, all right—talk!"

"I don't have your two quarters—"

"What'd you do?" demanded Arthur. "Spend 'em?"

"Never mind." Chelsea smiled sweetly. "I'll give you something better. I'll give you these goldfish!" She pointed to the glass jars.

"Huh?" repeated Arthur. He stared down at the red wagon as if he hadn't noticed it before. "You will? Both of 'em?"

Chelsea nodded. "Uh-huh."

"Hey, thanks! I didn't have time to get any goldfish at Family Fun Night. I had to leave early."

Arthur grinned and ambled off down the street, clutching the glass jars to his chest.

Chelsea grinned, too. She had to admit that she sort of liked goldfish, after all. But she liked them better when they belonged to someone else!

··11··

A Nasty Note

When it was time to walk to school the next morning, Mary Lynne gave Chelsea a cool "hello." Then, for a whole block, she didn't say another word.

Chelsea sighed. All weekend she'd been wondering what would happen today. "Are you still mad?" she asked Mary Lynne, "just because I told Arthur that Abigail didn't want to be his girlfriend?"

"I'm not mad, exactly, but you weren't very nice to Abigail. You should have told her!"

"I didn't think she'd care," muttered Chelsea. Then she changed the subject. "Wait till you hear what happened to the goldfish!" Chelsea explained about the mix-up at the neighborhood meeting, and pretty soon Mary Lynne was chattering away as usual.

But as soon as they stepped onto the school grounds, Mary Lynne spotted Abigail. "Come on," she called, "let's go jump rope!"

Chelsea set her lips in a stubborn, straight line. "I don't want to jump rope with Abigail!"

Mary Lynne put her hands on her hips. "You're still not being very nice, Chelsea. She didn't do anything to you. You did something to *her*."

Chelsea stuck out her lower lip. "I did not! How could I know that Abigail would be interested in what old Arthur had to say!"

Mary Lynne shrugged. "Well, I'm going to go over there with Abigail and jump rope. Come if you want to."

Mary Lynne ran off and left Chelsea standing all by herself. It just goes to show, thought Chelsea, that Mary Lynne likes Abigail better than me!

Chelsea's shoulders slumped. Sadly, she stared down at the ground, which had been soaked by an overnight rain. With the toe of her tennis shoe, she drew a Mr. Yuk face in the moist dirt. Then she found a stick and wrote A-B-I-G-A-I-L below it.

She smiled at her drawing before she rubbed it out. Everything is Abigail's fault! Chelsea told herself. I wish she'd never moved to this school!

The bell rang. On her way inside, Chelsea saw Mary Lynne and Abigail with their heads together, whispering. I'll bet they're talking about me, she thought.

She sat at her desk in the classroom, churning with anger. It wasn't fair, none of it was fair!

She tore a scrap of looseleaf out of her binder. *Do you like Abigail?* she wrote, and signed her name. Then she folded the paper three times.

She crouched low over her desk and whispered to Katie Klein. "Psst!"

Katie turned her head. Chelsea dropped the folded note on the floor and pushed it across the aisle with her foot. Katie looked straight ahead while she reached down and fumbled for the paper with one hand.

Still keeping one eye on the teacher, Katie picked up the note and read it. Then she wrote something on the back and passed it to Chelsea.

I don't know. Do you? Katie had written.

No! Chelsea wrote. She hesitated, then added, *I think she has a big nose.*

As she passed the note back again to Katie, Chelsea began to feel more cheerful. Abigail didn't really have a big nose, but it felt good to say so.

Katie read the message and started to giggle. She put her hands over her mouth so Mrs. Findlay wouldn't hear.

Chelsea grinned. But what was Katie doing now? Instead of sending the note back to Chelsea, she was tapping Lucy Burnett on the shoulder. When Lucy turned her head, Katie slipped her the scrap of paper.

This is awful! thought Chelsea. Katie wasn't supposed to pass the note around! "Psst!" she whispered to Katie. "Get my note back!"

Katie nodded.

Now Mrs. Findlay was calling the class to order. "Settle down, class. Get out your spelling workbooks."

Chelsea got out her workbook. At the same time,

she watched anxiously to see what was happening to her note.

Katie whispered to Lucy. But Lucy didn't pay any attention, or else she didn't hear Katie. Instead of returning Chelsea's message, Lucy was passing it on to Beverly Ann!

Chelsea tried to get Lucy's attention. "Hey," she said in a loud whisper, "don't give her that paper!"

Mrs. Findlay had been writing spelling words on the blackboard. She suddenly turned around and surveyed the class, searching for the source of the whispers. Chelsea hunched down in her seat.

The teacher turned back to the board. Chelsea sat upright again. She could see that Beverly Ann, with a smirk on her face, was already scanning the note. It would be just like Beverly Ann, Chelsea thought in alarm, to. . .to do something drastic!

Beverly Ann rolled the note into a ball. She held it in her hand close to the floor, then let it drop. Casually, she stuck out her foot and pushed the ball across the aisle.

"Psst!" whispered Beverly Ann, and Abigail turned around.

Beverly Ann was actually doing it—*she was passing the note to Abigail!* Chelsea felt sick; her stomach was churning. But what could she do?

While Abigail unfolded the paper, Chelsea watched anxiously. Abigail read the words that Chelsea had written and made a small noise—a sort of squeak. The back of her neck turned crimson.

Chelsea slumped down in her seat. Now I've done it, she thought. When I wrote that note, I didn't mean for Abigail to see it. She's going to be my enemy for life!

What was going to happen next?

Mrs. Findlay had finished with the list of spelling words. She was tapping her foot and darting annoyed looks at Abigail. Oh, no! thought Chelsea. Did that mean the teacher had seen the note?

"Abigail!" snapped Mrs. Findlay.

"Yes?"

"Do you have something you'd like to share with the class?"

Abigail shook her head.

"I mean," Mrs. Findlay said sternly, "that little piece of paper I saw you poring over a moment ago. Stand up, please, and read it aloud.''

Uh-oh! thought Chelsea. Here it comes!

Her heart began to pound—thump, thump, thump! And she had the same sensation in her stomach that she felt whenever she rode the Scrambler at the amusement park.

Abigail stumbled to her feet, looking quite miserable. "Uh...," she began in a choked voice.

This is all my fault, Chelsea told herself. She sank down even farther, so that now she could hardly see over the edge of her desk.

"Go ahead," said Mrs. Findlay.

Abigail twisted a corner of the paper. "It says...it says somebody has a big nose!"

Mrs. Findlay seemed surprised. "Are you sure that's what it says?"

Suddenly, Abigail's face changed. "No." She shook her head. "Actually, it says that Chelsea Martin has a big nose!"

What! Chelsea couldn't believe it. That wasn't what the note said. Abigail was lying!

"A big nose!" murmured Thomas. "Hah!"

Someone across the room snickered. And before

Chelsea knew it, everyone in the class was laughing. Laughing at *her*.

"All right, class," said Mrs. Findlay. "That's enough. Chelsea and Abigail, I want to see both of you after school."

··12··

The Peanut Butter Predicament

It was fifteen minutes after three. School was over, and everyone in third grade had gone home—everyone except Chelsea and Abigail.

"Now, girls," said Mrs. Findlay, who was perched on a corner of her desk. "I want to get to the bottom of this note business." She looked sternly at Abigail. "First of all, who wrote it? Was it you, Abbie?"

"No!" declared Abigail. "It was Chelsea—she wrote it about *me*!" Abigail put a hand up to touch her nose, as if she were checking its size. "And that's not all. She said she didn't like me!"

Mrs. Findlay turned to Chelsea. "Is that true?"

Without looking up at the teacher, Chelsea gave a little nod.

"I can hardly believe it," said Mrs. Findlay. "Writing that note wasn't a nice thing to do. That's not like you, Chelsea. Not at all."

Chelsea squirmed. I wish Mrs. Findlay would just yell at me, she thought, instead of trying to make me feel like a rotten person.

She twisted the hem of her sweatshirt. Writing those things about Abigail *was* pretty mean. "I'm sorry," she muttered.

Mrs. Findlay went on and on about the importance of something she called *courtesy*. Chelsea figured out that it meant kindness and good manners, and she felt embarrassed that her teacher thought she didn't have enough of it.

Finally, Mrs. Findlay let the two girls go. Abbie was out the front door in a minute, but Chelsea lingered at her locker. She felt awful.

I wasn't the only one who was rotten, she told herself. Abigail made me look bad in front of Mrs. Findlay. In fact, she's been causing trouble for me ever since she showed up at Avalon Elementary.

I wish she'd never come to this school, Chelsea thought again as she stomped down the hallway. She couldn't wait to get home; she had a plan to get even.

Mrs. Findlay had said it wasn't nice to write a nasty note *about* someone. But Chelsea was not going to do that. She was going to go straight home and write Abigail a letter—an angry letter!— telling her exactly what she thought of her.

And then...then she would march right over to Abigail's house and shove the letter into her hands. There! she'd say, read that!

As soon as she got home, Chelsea found some paper and a pencil. She sat down at her desk and began to write.

She bore down so hard on her pencil she made a hole in the paper. *I think you are a...a...a what?*

What word could she use? Not a really bad one—Chelsea wasn't allowed to swear. But there must be some name she could call Abigail, something that would let Abbie know how angry she was.

While Chelsea was running through all the

possibilities in her mind, a certain term popped into her head. It was an expression she'd heard her mother use once, when another car driver suddenly swerved in front of her.

Chelsea smiled. It was the perfect word. She licked her pencil tip and began to write.

When the letter was finished, Chelsea signed her name in cursive. She stuck the letter into an envelope, licked the flap, and pounded it down with her fist. Bam!

I'll take it over to Abigail's house right now, Chelsea decided. I'll ring the doorbell, and... what then?

Chelsea pictured herself tossing the letter at Abigail's feet and then stalking off. Or maybe smacking her with it, as if she were challenging Abigail to a duel. "Take that!" she would say. Whap! Whap!

When her mother wasn't home, Chelsea was supposed to check in after school with her next-door neighbor. She told Mrs. DeCastro that she was going to be playing outside for a while.

Ten minutes later, she was actually standing

on the MacCready front porch. And then she began to change her mind.

What would happen after she handed Abigail the letter? Would Abigail get angry? Yell? Make a fuss?

With her hands deep in the pockets of her denim jacket, Chelsea stood on the porch, thinking. What should she do?

She could do what the UPS delivery person did with packages. She could leave the envelope stuck between the two doors.

Squ-u-eak! went the hinges when Chelsea opened the storm door. She propped up the letter, and then—suddenly!—the other door moved. Someone had just yanked it open!

"Chelsea!" said a voice.

Chelsea jumped. Abigail was standing right there!

"Uh...hello," Chelsea said.

The envelope had fallen to the floor, right at Abigail's feet. I'm in trouble now, thought Chelsea. Abigail's going to pick up the letter and read it before I have a chance to get away!

But Abigail wasn't paying any attention to the letter. She seemed sort of upset. Her face was flushed. Wisps of red hair had come loose from her ponytail and were trailing down beside her ears.

"Am I ever glad to see you!" said Abigail.

Huh? What is she talking about? wondered Chelsea. This must be some kind of trick. After all, I wrote a nasty note about her just this morning! Why would she be glad to see me?

Chelsea didn't know what to say. Wishing that she could just disappear, she took a step backwards.

But Abigail grabbed Chelsea's arm. "Don't go, Chelsea! You've got to help me!" Chelsea was too surprised to resist, and Abigail pulled her inside the house.

Something strange was going on! Now Chelsea noticed that Abigail had gooey globs of brown stuff stuck to her hair. She sniffed. It was peanut butter!

"You've got to help me!" Abigail repeated. "I'll even...even pay you!"

"You mean," said Chelsea slowly, "you want to hire me to do a job for you?"

Abigail shrugged. "Well, sort of. Only, I'll

help, too." She pulled Chelsea through the living room and into the kitchen. "Look!"

In the middle of the kitchen floor sat Abigail's little brother. His chubby hands dabbled in a pool of something dark and sticky-looking, which he'd smeared not only over his clothes but on his face and hair, too.

Beside him was a large jar of peanut butter and an empty bottle of cooking oil. Nearby, a kitchen canister lay upside-down on a small mountain of flour.

"How did it happen?" asked Chelsea.

Abigail looked guilty. "He was taking a nap, so I went downstairs for a minute to watch TV. When I came up to check on him, I found him like this. He must have climbed out of his crib!"

Chelsea glanced around the kitchen. "Where's your mother?"

"That's the problem! Mom had a headache, so she went up to her room to lie down. She said to come get her if Brian woke up, but I don't want to go get her *now*. Not with the kitchen looking like this."

Brian raised his head and grinned. Then he stood up awkwardly. He went over to Abigail and threw his arms around her legs, leaving sticky, brown marks.

Abigail sighed. "We have safety latches on all the cupboard doors." Abigail pulled on a door to demonstrate. "But this one is broken!"

She turned to Chelsea. "If I don't get this mess cleaned up before Mom gets up, I'll be in big trouble! Will you help me, Chelsea?"

Why should I help her? thought Chelsea. She's my enemy! And it would serve her right to get in trouble.

But Abigail was staring at her in a way that made Chelsea feel guilty. "Come on. Please! I can't do it all myself!" she pleaded.

Oh! Chelsea thought, I don't know what to do!

··13··

Chelsea to the Rescue!

Chelsea looked at the kitchen floor. It was a terrible, awful mess! And Abigail's little brother was just as grubby. How could she walk out the door and leave Abigail in this predicament?

Besides, Chelsea remembered, Abigail had said she would pay. And a job was a job.

"All right," said Chelsea. "I'll stay. What do you want me to do?"

"Oh, good!" Abigail grabbed a big roll of paper towels from the counter. "Could you start wiping up the floor? I'll take Brian into the bathroom and get him cleaned up."

"Okay." Chelsea ripped a paper towel off the roll.

Oooh! Her feet made sucking noises when she walked on the sticky floor. I think I'll have to wet these towels, she decided. And I'll need to use a broom and dustpan to sweep up that flour.

After a few minutes, Chelsea surveyed the room. The floor was still tacky, and there were gobs of peanut butter lying around here and there. But the place looked a lot better.

Then Chelsea heard a brief cry coming from another room. She decided to find out what was the matter.

After trying a couple doors, she found the bathroom. "What's wrong?" she said. "Why did he yell like that?"

Abigail seemed even more flustered now than she had earlier. She was sitting on the toilet with her squirming brother in her lap. "I hope Mom didn't hear him," she said. "I tried to give him a shower. But when I turned on the water, he started to scream."

"You mean, taking a shower scares him?" asked Chelsea.

"I don't know. It's always Mom or Dad who

cleans him up." Abigail seemed very worried. "What can we do? I can't get his hair clean with just a washcloth."

Chelsea thought hard. "Well, what if. . .what if we got in the shower with him?"

Abigail frowned. "What do you mean? We're too old to take showers with other people! Besides, I don't want to get *my* hair wet—it takes too long to dry."

"I know! We could hold umbrellas over our heads," said Chelsea, "and wear bathing suits. Do you have an extra suit?"

"Yes!" said Abigail. "Quick—let's change!"

When they were ready, Chelsea glanced at herself in the bathroom mirror. The extra suit was one that Abigail had outgrown, but it fit Chelsea just right.

They closed the bathroom door so the shower noise wouldn't disturb Abigail's mother. Then Chelsea and Abigail each took one of Brian's hands and stepped into the shower enclosure. With her thumb, Abigail pressed a button on her umbrella handle. Pop! went the umbrella, opening wide.

Chelsea turned on the water. Immediately,

Brian screwed up his little face, ready to howl.

"Don't cry, Brian," said Abigail.

"It's all right," said Chelsea. "See?"

Brian looked up at the two girls, and his expression changed. He started to smile.

"Hey!" Abigail put a dab of baby shampoo on Brian's head. "It worked."

"Mm-hmm," said Chelsea. "That warm water feels good, doesn't it, Brian?"

Brian sat down. He patted the water around him and then chuckled with delight when it splashed.

Abigail gave a tiny kick and made a splash, too. "You know," she said, "this reminds me of something."

Chelsea turned around, and the warm drops pounded gently on her back. "What?"

"There's an old movie my parents like— it's called 'Singin' in the Rain.' It was on Channel 22 a few days ago. Did you see it?"

"Yeah, part of it," said Chelsea. "A man dances in a puddle and gets all wet, even though he has an umbrella?"

"Yeah, that's it. Why don't we do the same

thing? We can pretend we're in the movie."

Chelsea stared in amazement. Abigail wanted to prance around in the shower, crooning an old movie tune? She must be crazy! But on the other hand, it did sound like fun! "Okay."

"I'm sing-in' in the rain!" Abigail twirled her umbrella. Then Chelsea joined in. "Sing-in' in the rain..." Kick! Kick! Splash! Splash!

Little Brian clapped his hands and laughed.

"He likes it!" said Abigail. "Let's do it again."

Chelsea and Abigail opened their mouths wide. "I'm sing-in' in the—"

Suddenly, the bathroom door opened. Standing in the doorway, goggling at them, was Abigail's mother!

Uh-oh! thought Chelsea.

But Mrs. MacCready smiled. "Well, I don't know what's going on, but you look like you're having fun!"

"Yeah, we are." Abigail laughed. "Are you feeling better? Oh! And this is Chelsea."

"Hello," said Abigail's mother as she reached for a towel. "Yes, I'm feeling better. I see Brian woke up, too. It was nice of you two to bathe him. Now I won't have to do it later."

Abigail and Chelsea glanced at each other and began to giggle.

Mrs. MacCready wrapped her son in the towel. "After you've changed, girls, I'll find you a snack."

The kitchen floor was still a little sticky, but Abigail's mother didn't seem to notice. "How about pretzels and milk?" she asked.

For a while, Chelsea and Abigail ate in silence. Chelsea felt a little awkward and shy. She wasn't sure what to talk about. And just for a moment, she wondered what she was doing there with Abigail.

But then Abigail asked Chelsea something about the science homework. And soon they were chatting away about the bean experiment their class was doing.

"My seedling doesn't stand up straight," said Abigail. "It keeps leaning over sideways."

"Well," said Chelsea, "maybe it's tired!"

They both started to laugh. Abigail had just taken a sip of her drink; she sputtered, and a little bit of milk came out her nose! Then they couldn't stop laughing!

After a while, Chelsea looked up at the wall clock above the sink. "I'm supposed to be home by four-thirty. I'd better go now."

Abigail walked with Chelsea to the front door. "Wait a minute," she said, "and I'll get some money. I said I'd pay you for helping me."

Chelsea shook her head. "You don't have to pay me. It was fun."

"Do you mean it?"

"Uh-huh." It *was* fun, thought Chelsea— a lot of fun. And the peculiar thing was that she'd had a good time with Abigail MacCready— the girl she'd thought she hated!

"Maybe," said Abigail, "you and Mary Lynne could both come home from school with me tomorrow. Want to?"

"Yes." Chelsea added shyly, "And I'm sorry about what happened with Arthur. I should have told you about it—that he wanted you to be his girlfriend, I mean."

"Oh, forget it." Abigail tossed her head.

"I don't want to be his girlfriend, anyway!"

"Really?" said Chelsea. "Good!"

"Well, see you!" said Abigail, opening the door. "Hey! What's this?" She stooped and picked up a long, white envelope from the doorstep.

"Oh!" said Chelsea. Her letter to Abigail— she'd forgotten all about it!

"Don't read that!"

"Why not? It has my name on it."

"I know, but you shouldn't pay any attention to it. I wrote it when I was angry. And...and I called you a name."

Abigail frowned. "You did?"

"Ye-es."

Abigail ripped open the envelope.

Chelsea sighed. Now Abbie's going to be mad at me all over again, she thought. And just when we were getting to be friends.

Abigail held the paper in front of her, muttering the words half-aloud. "Dear Abigail, I think you are a..."

Why, oh why, thought Chelsea, did I ever write that letter?

Abigail continued slowly. "A *crum-bum!*"

Chelsea stared at her, waiting for an explosion.

But Abigail was smiling! "A crum-bum? Oh, Chelsea, that's a silly word!"

"It is?" Chelsea thought a minute. "Maybe that's what we should call Arthur."

Abigail nodded. "Good idea!" She tossed the letter in the wastebasket. "Well, I'll see you tomorrow!"

"Okay, see you!" Chelsea hopped down the porch steps and turned to wave at Abigail. "Oh!" she said, "and one more thing—your nose isn't big at all!"

"Neither is yours!" called Abigail.

I should have believed Mary Lynne, Chelsea thought, as she skipped along the sidewalk. She told me Abigail was nice!

··14··

No More Green

Later that afternoon, Chelsea talked on the telephone with her father. "Now tell me," he said, "how's the feud going?"

Chelsea was puzzled. "What do you mean?"

"I'm talking about the battle between you and that new girl at school—Abigail, is that her name?"

"O-o-oh," said Chelsea. "We're friends now."

"Really? How did that happen?"

Chelsea wound the telephone cord around her finger. "Well, it's hard to explain." In fact, it was a little hard for Chelsea to remember why she had ever disliked Abigail.

I was worried that Mary Lynne would choose Abigail as her best friend instead of me, she thought. That was silly; we can all three be friends. Hey!—just like the Three Musketeers.

"I think," Chelsea told her father, "I decided I didn't like her before I even got to know her."

"Oh!" said Mr. Martin. "And then, when you spent some time with her, it turned out that you *did* like her. Right?"

"Uh-huh."

"I know what that's like. I had a similar experience recently."

"You did?" Chelsea tried to picture her father feuding with another grownup.

"Yes. It happened last Saturday evening. I was invited to dinner at my friend Mike's house, and he and his wife served a delicious-looking casserole. It had tomato sauce, cheese, and mushrooms in it."

"Oh, I bet you liked that," said Chelsea. "It sounds almost like pizza."

"Yes," said Mr. Martin. "There were other ingredients, too, and the whole thing tasted wonderful! I ate a lot. So, you see?"

"No." Chelsea was puzzled. "That story doesn't have anything to do with Abigail and me.

It doesn't have anything to do with disliking someone before you get to know her."

"Yes, it does!" he said. "Because the casserole was eggplant parmigiana!"

"What!" Chelsea couldn't believe it. Her father had eaten eggplant and *liked* it!

Mr. Martin laughed. "Yes!"

Just then Chelsea's mother came into the kitchen. "Mary Lynne's here, Chelsea. She said she wanted to talk to you for just a minute."

"I've gotta go now, Dad," said Chelsea. "Bye!"

Mary Lynne was waiting in the living room. "I can only stay a second," she said. "My mom's out in the car."

"Okay," said Chelsea.

"I just wanted to tell you—I saw Abigail at the library, and she and I had an idea. All three of us could wear our green shirts to school tomorrow, and then we'll be dressed alike. Okay?"

"Oh," said Chelsea, "that's a good idea!"

After Mary Lynne left, Chelsea went to check her closet. She wanted to make sure her shirt was clean.

Oh, darn! The shirt was in the laundry hamper with a spot of gravy on the front. Chelsea took it into the bathroom. She didn't want to disappoint Mary Lynne and Abigail. Maybe she could wash out the stain.

Chelsea reached for the small bottle of detergent her mother kept in the bathroom. After squirting a bit on the spot, she began to rub.

She stared down at the sudsy green shirt. The color reminded her of something.

St. Patrick's Day!—and the green marker she'd used to tint her skin. Then she remembered Beverly Ann had said green is the color of envy—of jealousy.

Chelsea looked up. She peered into the mirror. With wide eyes, she gazed long and hard at her reflection. Then she grinned. Good! There wasn't a bit of green left on her face—not a single speck!

BECKY THOMAN LINDBERG lives in Baltimore, Maryland, with her husband, son, and daughter, as well as a dog and two cats. Besides writing, she enjoys art; she paints landscapes and portraits in oils and pastels.

As a child, Mrs. Lindberg read many books and occasionally wrote stories of her own. Both *Speak Up, Chelsea Martin!* and *Chelsea Martin Turns Green* were inspired by her childhood memories and by the adventures of her daughter, Carolyn.